The Secret Egg

Written by
John Townsend

Illustrated by
Ian David Marsden

I'll tell you such a secret,
but please don't make a fuss.
For I found something very strange
when I caught the morning bus.

Just there beside me on the seat,
pressed warm against my leg,
was something rugby ball in shape …
a large, green speckly egg.

I took it home and kept it warm,
snug beneath the cat.
He stirred and purred, then raised a paw
and gave the egg a pat.

He dabbed at it and gave a sigh,
rolled over on his back,
then shut his eyes and went to sleep …
as the shell began to crack.

Slowly, through a tiny hole
which grew across the egg,
I saw a scaly face pop out
and one green scaly leg.

Chip, crack; chip, crack; chip, crack; chip, crack.
In place of yellow yolk,
red eyes peeped out above long jaws
that blew a puff of smoke.

I heard the tiniest of sounds,
like chip, chip from a chisel.
Then bits of broken shell flew off,
with hiss, and fizz, and sizzle!

A cloud of orange smoke burst out
that smelt of spicy mustard …
and then a spurt of pinkish slime
that looked like strawberry custard.

The room began to shake and quake.
The sofa twanged and quivered,
for there before my very eyes,
a baby was delivered!

This was no ordinary chick;
it wasn't like a bird.
There was no chirping, nor a squawk …
instead, a voice was heard.

There were no words that I could tell;
just murmurs, then a pause.
I whispered back, "Hello, my friend,"
and stroked its tiny claws.

The cat slept on without a care,
just opening half an eye,
as little stretchy wings emerged
with a smoky, sparky sigh.

Next came a sneeze and snuffly sniffs,
then lots of yelpy barks.
The little mouth with dribbly tongue
coughed out bright purple sparks.

The cat looked startled and surprised
and gave his tail a flick.
He stretched his neck to sniff the 'thing'
and gave a friendly lick.

The baby dragon's grown a lot.
My cat's its closest friend.
Their story's only just begun …
who knows where it will end?